The Farmer's Rat

Written by
Michelle Larbey

Illustrated by
Juliet Breese

02398

Badger Publishing Limited
Suite G08
Business & Technology Centre
Bessemer Drive
Stevenage, SG1 2DX
www.badger-publishing.co.uk
enquiries@badger-publishing.co.uk

The Farmer's Rat

Text © Michelle Larbey 2010
Complete work © Badger Publishing Limited 2010

ISBN 978 1 84926 188 3

Publisher: David Jamieson
Editor: Danny Pearson
Design: Fiona Grant
Illustration: Juliet Breese

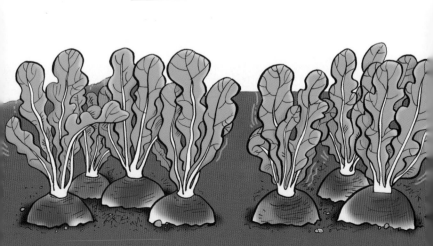

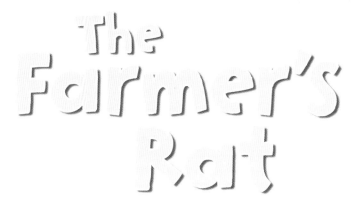

The Farmer's Rat

Written by
Michelle Larbey

Illustrated by
Juliet Breese

Badger Publishing

New words:

exclaimed   enormous

amazement   delicious

manure

Meet the main characters:

Farmer

Farmer's wife

The rat

There was once a farmer
who loved to grow and sell
delicious vegetables.

The people in the village
loved to buy his juicy
vegetables.

However, one morning the farmer noticed something terrible had happened to all his crops.

All of the vegetables had great big holes in them and the leaves were floppy and pale.

"Oh no!" exclaimed the farmer. "Nobody is going to buy our vegetables now."

"We have no money left so we will have to sell our lovely home," cried the farmer's wife.

But that night, when the farmer and his wife went to bed, something magical happened to the turnips.

12

"How on earth did they grow so big?" said the puzzled farmer in the morning.

"Look!" said the farmer's wife, "they have no holes in them."

The next day, the farmer went outside only to find the biggest potatoes he had ever seen.

"I don't understand," said the farmer to his wife, "how did they grow so big?"

"Why don't we stay up all night and find out what is happening?" said his wife.

Later that night, just after the stroke of midnight the farmer and his wife peeped out from behind the curtains.

To their amazement they watched a little rat running around...

...sprinkling the radishes
with something whilst singing
a little song...

"I'm sure I can cure ...

with this lovely manure."

Suddenly the radishes grew
and grew and grew and all
the insects said "phooey"...

...and ran away from the terrible smell.

Once the rat had finished, he yawned and plodded back to his hole to get some sleep.

The next morning the farmer
and his wife sold the enormous
vegetables for lots of money.

No longer needing to sell
their lovely home they
thought of a way to thank
the rat.

That night the farmer built
the rat his very own home...

...and the farmer's wife knitted him some warm clothes.

From that day on, they all
lived happily ever after,
eating delicious vegetables
every day.

Questions

Once you have read this book and talked about the pictures, have a go at answering these questions...

What did the farmer and his wife grow?

Tell me what happened to the farmer's vegetables.

What did the rat sing as he spread manure on to the radishes?

How did the famer and his wife thank the rat?

Describe your favourite vegetable.